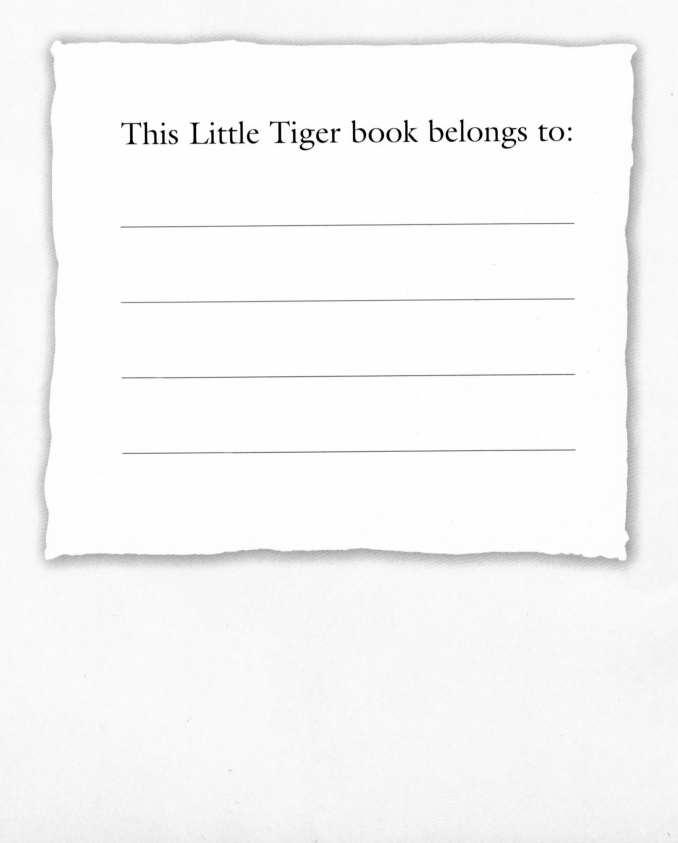

This Little Tiger book belongs to:

_____

_____

_____

_____

In Memory of Michael Murphy
~ M.C.

For Mom & Dad
~ G.W.

LITTLE TIGER PRESS
An imprint of Magi Publications
1 The Coda Centre, 189 Munster Road,
London SW6 6AW, UK
www.littletigerpress.com
First published in Great Britain 1994
by Little Tiger Press, London
This edition published 2008

LAZY OZZIE

Michael Coleman

Pictures by

Gwyneth Williamson

LITTLE TIGER PRESS

Ozzie was a very lazy owl.

"It's time you
learned to fly,"
said Mother Owl
one day.
But Ozzie said,
"Oh, do I have to?"
He didn't want to learn to fly. All that
wing-flapping looked like too much hard work.
Ozzie's favorite thing to do was
to sit around.
"I'm practicing being wise,"
he said.

"Well, I want you to fly,"
said his mother sternly.
"Now, I'm going out to look
for some food. And if you *are* wise,
you will be on the ground by the time I come back!"

Ozzie thought hard.

If he was wise, then he should be able to think of a way of getting down to the ground without flying.

Suddenly he noticed the horse who lived in their barn. The horse's head came up almost as high as the beam Ozzie was sitting on.

Ozzie had an idea . . .

"Help, help!" he yelled.
"What's the matter?" asked
the high horse.

"It's an emergency!" cried Ozzie, jumping onto the high horse's back. "Take me to the milk shed!"

So the high horse took Ozzie to the milk shed.

In the milk shed there lived a cow who wasn't quite as high as the high horse.

"It's an emergency!" cried Ozzie, jumping onto the not-quite-so-high cow's back. "Take me to the pigsty!"

So the high horse and the not-quite-so-high cow took Ozzie to the pigsty.

In the pigsty there lived a pig. The pig wasn't as tall as the not-quite-so-high cow. But he was a big pig.

"It's an emergency!" cried Ozzie, jumping onto the big pig's back. "Take me to the barnyard!"

So the high horse,
the not-quite-so-high cow
and the big pig took Ozzie
to the barnyard.

In the barnyard there lived a sheepdog.
The sheepdog wasn't as tall as the big pig.
He was a short sheepdog.
"It's an emergency!" cried Ozzie,
jumping onto the short sheepdog's back.
"Take me to the pasture!"

So the high horse,
the not-quite-so-high cow,
the big pig and the short
sheepdog took Ozzie to
the pasture.

In the pasture there lived a lamb. The lamb wasn't as tall as the short sheepdog. She was a little lamb. "It's an emergency!" cried Ozzie, jumping onto the little lamb's back.

"Take me to the duck pond!"

So the high horse, the not-quite-so-high cow, the big pig, the short sheepdog and the little lamb took Ozzie to the duck pond.

In the duck pond there lived a duck. The duck wasn't as tall as the little lamb. He was a dinky duck. "It's an emergency!" cried Ozzie, jumping onto the dinky duck's back. "Take me to the barn!"

So the high horse, the not-quite-so-high cow, the big pig, the short sheepdog, the little lamb and the dinky duck took Ozzie back to the barn.

As soon as they got there, Ozzie hopped down
to the ground from the dinky duck's back.
He'd done it!
Now that's what you call being wise,
he told himself!

"So what's the emergency?" asked the high horse.
"Oh," said Ozzie. "I was only kidding.
Wasn't that fun?"

The high horse, the not-quite-so-high cow,
the big pig, the short sheepdog, the little lamb
and the dinky duck weren't amused.
They went away grumbling.
But Ozzie was happy. His plan had worked.
He was pretty wise already.

"I flew all the way down,"
he said proudly to his mother
when she came back.

Mother Owl gave a big smile.
"That's wonderful," she said.
Ozzie thought she was
pleased with him . . .

. . . but he didn't know
that she'd been watching
the whole time.
"Now let me see you fly
back up again," said
Mother Owl.

fantastic reads from Little Tiger Press

for information regarding any of the above titles
or for our catalogue, please contact us:
Little Tiger Press, 1 The Coda Centre,
189 Munster Road, London SW6 6AW, UK
Tel: +44 (0)20 7385 6333 Fax: +44 (0)20 7385 7333
E-mail: info@littletiger.co.uk www.littletigerpress.com